IMPORTAN'

To all the creatures in the Kingdom of Bellua

As the terrible threat posed by the wicked Imp King Ivar grows, I'm calling on you. He has already stolen magic from four of us – no one is safe from his attacks. With each power he gains, his strength increases.

Some of you have met our respected Guardian, Hattie B. When she next visits our land, we must come together to greet her. Only she can defeat the determined Ivar. She needs our help more than ever!

When you hear of the Guardian's arrival, make your way to her cave without delay. We cannot allow Ivar to seize power. Creatures of Bellua, heed my call!

Themis
Leader of the unicorns

Read all the adventures of

THE DRAGON'S SONG

THE UNICORN'S HORN

THE FAIRY'S WING

THE MERMAID'S TAIL

THE PONY'S HOOF

Don't miss

THE PHOENIX'S FLAME

Hattie B Magical Vet

The Pony's Hoof

CLAIRE TAYLOR-SMITH

Illustrated by Lorena Alvarez

PUFFIN

PUFFIN BOOKS

UK | USA | Canada | Ireland | Australia
India | New Zealand | South Africa

Puffin Books is part of the Penguin Random House group of companies whose
addresses can be found at global.penguinrandomhouse.com.

puffinbooks.com

First published 2015

001

Set in 14.5/24 pt Bembo Book MT Std
Typeset by Jouve (UK), Milton Keynes
Printed in Great Britain by Clays Ltd, St Ives plc

A CIP catalogue record for this book is available from the British Library

ISBN: 978-0-141-35244-2

www.greenpenguin.co.uk

With love to Dad, Tony and Trina

xxx

To my dear Mother Bear, with love

xxx

Winter Mountains

Cave

Valley
of the
Guardians

Dragon's
Valley

Pixie
Park

Elf Avenue

Silvery Stream

Unicorn
Meadows

Enchanted
Orchard

Rumbling
Volcano

Fairy Forest

Troll
Bridge

Rainbow
Waterfall

Ancient
Desert

Hidden
Lake

Frozen
Merlakes

Contents

Good Sports

It was the end of another school day and Hattie Bright and her best friend, Chloe, were the last to leave the classroom.

'Are you coming to Sports Club?' asked Hattie.

Chloe nodded as she lifted her red rucksack from her peg. 'Come on. We'd better get changed or we're going to be late!'

Hattie grabbed her own bag, and the two friends set off for the changing rooms, which were on the other side of the playground.

'Mr Kennedy said we can try whatever we like today,' said Chloe. 'What do you think you'll go for? I might do some throwing practice. I really want to get into the rounders team this year.'

Hattie thought for a moment. 'Hmmm, maybe running. Definitely not throwing – I'm *useless* at it!'

'That's why you need to practise!' said Chloe, laughing.

They were walking across the playground when they spotted a boy wandering around just ahead. First he crossed it in one direction, then another.

'Isn't that Rishi?' Hattie asked, recognizing the short dark hair of their new classmate. He had joined the school a couple of days ago.

Chloe nodded. 'He looks a bit lost,' she said. 'Let's go and see if he needs some help.'

However, as they walked towards him, the door of the girls' changing room flew open and out swept Victoria Frost. She was dressed in a pristine new sports kit. Beside her were her friends Jodie and Louisa, who were rarely far from Victoria's side.

'Hey, you, new boy!' called Victoria, striding towards Rishi. 'What *are* you doing?'

'I'm going to Sports Club,' Hattie heard Rishi reply, 'but I don't know where to get changed.'

'Hang on, I'll tell you!' Victoria shouted back, but Hattie saw a sneaky smile spread over her face. It looked like poor Rishi was in trouble.

Speeding up, Hattie reached him seconds after Victoria, who was already in full flow. Her sidekicks were sniggering beside her.

'Actually,' Victoria was saying, 'it's the same door for the girls' *and* boys' changing rooms. It's just that the sign saying *Boys* fell off at the end of last term. You go through the door that says *Girls*, and there are two more doors inside – one for girls and one for boys. You go through the boys' one. Obviously.'

Rishi opened his mouth to say thank you, but Hattie could feel fury rising up inside her.

'You know that's not true,' she said firmly to Victoria, stepping forward. She felt herself flush red at standing up to the unkind girl. 'I suppose you think it's funny to make Rishi walk into the girls' changing room because he's new? Well, it isn't. It's mean. All he wanted was some help.'

Victoria's mouth formed a surprised O, but for once she seemed lost for words.

'It was only a bit of fun,' she said eventually. 'Come on, Jodie, Louisa. Some people can't take a joke.'

Hattie breathed a sigh of relief as Victoria strode back to the girls' changing room. She turned to Rishi, who looked even more confused than before.

'You'll get used to Victoria,' said Hattie, not wanting to tell tales. 'Anyway, the boys' changing room is on the other side of the hall. If you walk past the main entrance, you'll spot a green door. I promise there's a sign on it saying *Boys*. It's stuck on perfectly.'

'Thanks,' said Rishi. 'I hope I haven't missed any of the club. I love sport! I used to be in nearly every team at my old school – we won loads of trophies.'

Hattie smiled. 'Don't worry. You'll be fine if you get changed quickly.'

Then she and Chloe rushed off to get ready too.

After getting changed, Hattie and Chloe were on their way to the sports field when Hattie noticed that one of her laces was undone. Telling Chloe to go ahead, she bent down to tie it – and that's when she saw the tell-tale glow of the charms on her special bracelet, which she never took off. The star, dragon, unicorn, fairy and mermaid charms had all turned a warm yellowy-orange colour. It meant only one thing: somewhere in the Kingdom of Bellua, a magical animal needed her help.

The evil King Ivar of the Imps must have stolen another magical power. Hattie counted on her fingers the powers that Ivar had already taken. He had a dragon's song to send his enemies to sleep, the magic from a unicorn's horn to control the weather, the ability to fly from a fairy's wing, and the colours from a mermaid's tail so he could blind his enemies and camouflage himself.

What power had he taken now?

There was no time to waste. Nobody else could help the poor creature and try to stop Ivar. She had to get to Bellua – and fast!

'I forgot my hairband!' she called to Chloe. To prove the point, she bunched up her long dark hair with its unusual white streak. 'I'll just run back and get one from my bag. Meet you on the field.'

While Chloe walked on, Hattie turned on her heels and sprinted straight to the school gate. She checked the coast was clear and ran home as quickly as she could.

In her bedroom, Hattie was panting as she pulled a dull leather vet's bag out from its hiding place under her bed. Opening the lock with her star charm, she watched as the bag turned a gorgeous sparkly silver. She traced over the glowing purple letters – *H* and *B* – that appeared on it, before leaning forward and peering inside. There was the beautiful

shell Marina the mermaid had given her on her last visit. That trip had ended with another successful cure, but Hattie couldn't help feeling a little worried that things might not go so well this time.

However, a rush of excitement about going back to Bellua soon helped Hattie to push any fears aside.

'I'm coming, Bellua!' she whispered, and immediately she felt herself tumbling down, down and down . . .

Telling Tales

Hattie was pleased to find her friend Mith Ickle in the Guardian's cave. The little pink dragon was perched on the stone table in the middle of the cave, delighted to see Hattie again. The crystal-studded walls glinted, and the shelves cut into them were loaded with pretty glass potion bottles. But something was different. Although the cave was usually silent, this time Hattie could hear a low murmur on the other side of the wooden door at the back.

'Hello, Mith!' cried Hattie. Then, lowering her voice slightly, she added, 'That's not who I think it is making all that noise, is it?'

'Ivar?' replied Mith Ickle. 'Oh no! I haven't spotted him lurking around . . . yet. Why don't you open the door? I kept it closed or you wouldn't have had anywhere to land!'

When Hattie threw open the door, she saw what Mith Ickle had meant. A huge crowd of creatures was gathered outside, jostling each other as they pressed closer. There was a cheer as they spotted the Guardian.

Hattie waved in surprise as she took in the amazing scene. Magical creatures of all shapes, sizes and shades mingled together in a sea of colours. While some animals stood on the soft velvety grass, above them fairies and sprites flitted, their shimmering wings creating sparks in Bellua's bright sky. Tiny pixies and imps peeped out between the legs of unicorns and trolls, and even the sphinxes were there. Hattie couldn't begin to count how many creatures had gathered to greet her.

Nor could she work out what any of them were saying! It seemed they all had a story to tell. Crouching down, she caught the end of a

pixie's description of how Ivar had tried to lull her to sleep with a song.

'I was only saved because I dozed off on a thorn. That woke me up pretty quickly!' explained the pixie with a grin.

Before Hattie could respond, a large dragon swooped by and told her he'd overheard Ivar making plans to steal his fire.

The high voices of the smaller creatures merged with the low voices of the larger ones, getting louder and louder . . . until suddenly the much deeper sound of an animal clearing his throat filled the air, and everyone went quiet. When this creature stepped through the crowd Hattie recognized him immediately. It was Themis, leader of the unicorns.

'My friends,' began Themis, addressing the crowd. 'Let us not all speak together. We must welcome our Guardian. She is here to help us defeat the evil King Ivar, whose wickedness is spreading further into our beautiful land.'

Themis then turned his majestic head to Hattie and spoke to her directly. 'What you have heard is true. Ivar has attempted to steal more of our precious magical powers. We are so thankful that you have come again to aid us in our struggle. And we want you to know that we will be here, if you need our help.'

There was a murmur of agreement from the assembled crowd and Hattie bowed her head in gratitude. She hoped she wouldn't let these wonderful creatures down.

'I'll do all I can to help you defeat Ivar,' she said when everyone fell silent again. Scanning the crowd before her, she asked, 'Does someone need my help now? Who has met Ivar today?'

There was movement in the gathering, then Hattie saw a small horse-like animal hobbling slowly towards the front. The creature was

apricot-coloured with silky, dark pink hair. At first Hattie thought it was another unicorn, but then she noticed the wings folded awkwardly by his side. Was it some kind of magical flying pony?

Hattie made her way to the young creature straight away and knelt down to examine him. However, the noise from the crowd began to build again, and she couldn't hear what he was saying.

She stood up and said aloud, 'Everyone, thank you so much for coming here, and for trusting me to help you. I will do my very best.' The creatures quietened down once more, so she added, 'I have to take this little one to my cave for treatment, but I really hope to meet you all again soon.'

Themis started off a chorus of goodbyes that sailed through Bellua's lightly shimmering sky as Hattie led the limping creature into the cave.

While Mith Ickle closed the wooden door behind them, Hattie reached for the big red book that she had used on her previous visits: *Healing Magickal Beastes & Creatures*. It had been used by generations of Guardians before her to find cures.

She turned to her patient and he looked up at her, his large plum-coloured eyes full of sadness.

'You poor little pony,' Hattie said gently. 'I know Ivar had something to do with this, but can you tell me exactly what happened? Then I'm sure I'll be able to help you.'

Hattie saw a tear form in the corner of one of the young creature's eyes and roll down his face. She put her fingers between his soft ears and gave him a soothing stroke.

The winged pony nuzzled against her, and Hattie could feel his small body trembling. Just what had Ivar done to terrify him and leave him barely able to walk? She listened carefully as he began his story.

A Sprinkle of Spice

The first thing the creature did was tell Hattie and Mith Ickle his name, which was Archeron. 'But you can call me Archie for short,' he said. Then he added, 'I'm a pegasus, you know.'

'Ah, so that's why you've got wings!' said Hattie, who had never come across one of these flying ponies in Bellua before.

She lifted Archie carefully on to the vet's table and peered closely at his front foot. It looked swollen and very painful.

'So, Archie, how did you hurt your hoof?' she asked, anxious to find a cure as quickly as possible.

'Well, I know it was a bit naughty, but I was practising my flying, even though my parents told me I was too young,' said Archie. 'I should only just be learning to open my wings.'

He demonstrated by jerkily spreading his wings, so that his fluffy feathers tickled Hattie's cheek.

'I'd managed to lift off the ground when I heard a scary noise, like really loud thunder or an

explosion!' continued Archie. 'Then there was some horrible loud laughing and . . . and . . .'

Archie's eyes filled with tears again, which this time fell freely down his face.

Hattie hugged the little pegasus until he stopped crying.

'Did you see Ivar?' she asked gently.

Archie shook his head. 'The sky turned grey and the shimmering colours disappeared and a loud wind whistled around me. It lifted me higher and higher and spun me round and round. I couldn't do anything – my wings were useless!'

Now Archie's trembling had turned to shaking and his soft furry ears were twitching nervously.

'Was it the spinning that injured your hoof?' Hattie asked.

Archie shook his head again. 'No. The wind stopped as suddenly as it began and I fell to the ground. I must have landed badly because when I looked at my hoof it was twisted and I couldn't walk on it. And I'm sure I heard that horrible laugh again when I tried.'

'So do you think Ivar was after your flying power?' Hattie asked, a little confused. Ivar had already stolen the power of flight from Titch the fairy. Why would he want it again?

'I think he might have wanted another pegasus power,' replied Archie. 'We can make springs of water appear from dry ground. We just need to stamp our hooves! It's quite useful if you need a drink. My cousin's so good at it that he can make a lake if he stamps enough. I think Ivar might have taken that power from me. I can't stamp my hoof to see because it hurts so much. It took me a while to get back to my family, but I made it in the end. They brought me here . . . and now they're waiting outside to see if you can help. So can you, Hattie B? Can you make my hoof better again?'

The hope in Archie's young eyes brought a lump to Hattie's throat. She had to find a magical cure and treat Archie as soon as possible. Then she might be able to protect Bellua from Ivar's evil plans.

Flicking through the red book, Hattie quickly found the page that dealt with pegasus injuries. At first, she could only see problems to do with wings: stiffness when opening, lost feathers and uneven flapping. Then, at the bottom of the page, she spotted a passage on leg injuries. Just below it there was a box on hooves, with a pretty border of twisted branches hung with horseshoes.

Hattie waited impatiently for all the text to magically appear on the page. One by one the words formed:

A twisted hoof is cured by eating a twistabout apple (cut in the very thinnest of slices).

Below was a picture of a large apple, coloured in with gold ink. Hattie had never seen such a grand illustration in the red book before. She thought it must be a very special apple indeed!

A twisted hoof is cured by eating a twistabout apple
-·-(Cut in the very thinnest of slices)-·-

As Hattie read on, she learned that the fruit only grew at the top of one tree in the Enchanted Orchard. It was the Great Twister Tree, which the book described as having '*the twistiest of branches and the palest of leaves*'.

'Let's hope I can find the tree, Mith,' said Hattie, as further instructions appeared on the page. 'Oh, look! The book's telling me more about the apple – and there's a rhyme too. Listen.'

Hattie read the rhyme aloud, her forehead wrinkled in concentration:

A Guardian's hand alone may touch this cure,
Or the apple's power exists no more.

Only once each year it grows to size.
If tainted or bruised, the whole tree dies.

'That's it! We need to go to the Enchanted Orchard!' Hattie said to Mith Ickle, who was hovering by her shoulder.

However, just as she was about to close the book, more text appeared. The writing was getting smaller and smaller in order to fit on the page, and she had to squint to read it.

For full and lasting recovery, sprinkle each apple piece with cinnamon spice from the honeyspice bees, and the pegasus will be able to summon water once more.

The idea of finding a mysterious tree, a special apple and this spice filled Hattie with excitement. She'd begun to look forward to the challenges that came with every adventure in Bellua – and she had Mith Ickle to help her along the way too.

A map fluttered out of the book, and Hattie caught it. She looked over to her loyal friend, who had flown across to the young pegasus. The little dragon was cheering Archie up by puffing out small rings of smoke from her nostrils. Hattie was sorry to interrupt their game but she knew they had to get going.

'Right, Mith,' she said, putting the trusty map in her pocket. 'Let's collect the spice first and find the apple in the Enchanted Orchard on the way back. And remember to watch out for Ivar. He's never far away when I'm around!'

Hattie helped Archie down from the table and led him outside. The crowd had gone now and only Archie's family remained by the entrance to Unicorn Meadows. The group of pegasi were hovering by the arch, their faces pinched with worry.

A large pegasus gracefully stepped forward and greeted them as they approached.

'I'm Arlon, Archie's father. I just want to say thank you, Guardian.'

'Don't worry – we'll have Archie better in no time,' said Hattie, guiding the little winged pony to his mother, who nudged him

protectively under her belly. 'We'll be back before you know it with the medicine he needs.'

As she strode through Unicorn Meadows with Mith Ickle alongside her, Hattie felt the weight of the challenge on her shoulders.

Flower Power

'Now where would I find a honeyspice bee?' Hattie wondered aloud.

The blank look on Mith Ickle's face told her the little dragon didn't know. Hattie had started to look around when a thought struck her: *Don't bees like flowers?* There were lots of flowers in Unicorn Meadows and she wondered if it would be a good place to start.

'Is this where I'll find the best flowers in Bellua?' she asked Mith Ickle, glancing around the meadow.

The dragon thought for a moment, then replied, 'Not really. The brightest ones grow in Pixie Park – it's full of them!'

'Then I reckon that's where we should head first. I can't see any bees around here anyway,' said Hattie, as she checked her map for the route. How she would collect spice from a bee was another problem, but she knew she'd think of something. Archie was relying on her.

It was a short walk to Pixie Park, but Hattie had to jump over several puddles on the way. Mith Ickle sensibly stayed in the air.

'Has it rained much here, Mith?' asked Hattie.

The little dragon shook her head.

Hattie remembered what Archie had said. 'Perhaps Ivar has been trying out his new power already . . .' Hattie's eyes darted around to see if the nasty imp was nearby, but she couldn't spot him.

The entrance to Pixie Park was marked by a huge garland of flowers, which formed the prettiest arch Hattie had ever seen. Hattie knew immediately that she'd come to the right place. Bursts of yellow, orange, purple and pink made her blink in wonder. The flowers were brighter than any she'd seen in her world. They were as luminous as the highlighter pens her parents used at their vet's practice. The arch had been clearly built for Bellua's smaller residents,

though, and Hattie had to duck to pass under it. Mith Ickle followed closely behind.

On the other side, Hattie's trainers sank into deep green grass, which smelled as sweet as a newly mown lawn. She looked around and was excited to see flowers blooming all over the park in bright clusters. Even better, a group of pixies were emerging from a nearby clump.

Hattie called out a friendly hello, then crouched down to speak to the tiny creatures. She felt Mith Ickle curl round her shoulders and wondered if the dragon was worried they would tease her as the fairies always did.

'You're Hattie, aren't you?' asked one rosy-cheeked pixie, who was dressed in a bright yellow outfit. 'Our friends saw you earlier. They said you're going to help us beat that horrible Imp King. We hope you can. He's already tried to steal our most magical flowers, you know.'

The five other pixies in the group shook their heads crossly.

'I'll do everything I can to help you all,' said Hattie. 'Actually, perhaps you can help me? Ivar has hurt a young pegasus who desperately needs special medicine. I'm looking for the honeyspice bees and I hoped they might be here.'

A second pixie stepped forward. 'Yes, the honeyspice bees do come here to enjoy

our beautiful flowers, but we never see them. They fly much too high for us to spot. We only know they're inside a flower when the petals close up and it starts buzzing. Then we stay well away. There's a famous pixie rhyme we all learn when we're very young . . .'

Hattie listened as all the pixies chanted together:

A buzzing flower is a dangerous thing,
For inside hides a bee with a sting!

A sting? The idea of being stung hadn't even occurred to Hattie. She remembered when Chloe had stepped on a bee in her garden and screamed so loudly that the next-door neighbour had come over to see if she was OK. She shivered slightly at the memory and felt Mith Ickle curl even tighter round her shoulders.

'Well, at least we're in the right place,' she said, putting all thoughts of stings out of her head.

Thanking the pixies for their help, Hattie stood up. 'We'll just have to wander around and look for them then,' she said. 'They've got to be here somewhere.'

Mith Ickle flew high in the clear blue sky and Hattie walked from one end of Pixie Park to the other, but they had no luck, and Hattie was beginning to get impatient as she thought of Archie in pain.

After several more minutes of searching, Hattie found Mith Ickle peering at a large clump of dazzling violet flowers with huge velvety petals.

'There must be a better way to . . .' Hattie began.

'To what?' asked Mith Ickle, but Hattie had wrinkled up her nose, and her eyes were fixed in concentration.

'Can you smell that?' she asked, turning to the little dragon.

Mith Ickle wrinkled up her own nose. 'Smell what?'

'Cinnamon! The book said the spice was cinnamon.'

'What's cinnamon?' asked Mith Ickle, looking puzzled.

'You know, it smells sort of — warm and, well, spicy. Like, um, hot cross buns and apple pie and, er, Christmas?'

The little dragon looked confused, but Hattie couldn't waste any more time with explanations.

'Follow me!' she said, holding her nose high in the air and breathing in deeply as she strode through the grass. She could smell the spice and it would lead her to the right place. She was sure of it.

The spicy smell grew stronger as Hattie walked. It made her think of the apple pancakes Dad sometimes made on Sunday mornings and the plum pudding that Grandma brought to their house every Christmas Eve.

Suddenly the smell grew so strong that Hattie's eyes watered, and a noisy buzzing filled her ears. A few metres in front of her was a swarm of several hundred tiny bees. They looked just like the bees she often saw in her garden at home, although these ones had bright blue stripes! She'd found the honeyspice bees at last.

Smells and Sounds

Hattie was so excited that she raced after the bees without a thought. They led her through Pixie Park and she soon found herself at the rocky outer edges of Dragon's Valley. She was joined by a wheezing Mith Ickle. The dragon was blowing out small puffs of smoke after racing to keep up with her.

They both watched open-mouthed as the swarm of bees separated into several neat lines and made their way towards a rocky outcrop. There were several hives and each was an oval shape about the size of a rugby ball. They were

the same brilliant blue colour as the bees' stripes. Hattie noticed they glowed brighter each time a bee entered. It was as if the hive was welcoming the bees back. Could the bees really be as dangerous as the pixies said they were?

When the last bee had disappeared into its hive, Hattie felt ready to creep a bit closer. Yet the hives were just out of her reach. She tried placing her feet on small ledges of rock and pushing herself up, but her trainers kept slipping and the rough rock scraped her hands.

'Let me help,' said Mith Ickle, and she flew up to take a look.

'There's something covering the top of the hive, like a powder,' the little dragon reported as she swooped back down and perched beside Hattie at the foot of the rocks. 'Smells a bit funny, though.'

'A bit – cinnamon-like?' asked Hattie hopefully. 'That *must* be what I have to collect! There has to be a way for me to get up there.'

Mith Ickle fluttered up again and tried to collect some of the powder for Hattie, but her claws got in the way. Then she tried pushing a pile together with her snout, but she kept sneezing and blowing it away!

'Oh dear!' Hattie exclaimed. 'Maybe I can find something to stand on.' But there didn't seem to be anything nearby that she could move into the right position.

'I've got it!' yelled Mith Ickle suddenly.

She swooped down and picked up a long reed with a spongy end and gave it to Hattie.

'You reach up and sweep the powder with this. I'll go up by the hive and guide you to carefully push the spice into this nutshell,' she said, holding up a shell that she had spotted on the ground.

'Brilliant, Mith!' said Hattie. 'And I won't have to get too close to the bees either. I don't know what I'd do without you!'

The little dragon beamed as she flew up, watching her friend point the reed nervously towards the top of one of the beehives.

The buzzing sound was quiet at first, but, when Hattie guided the reed closer to the top of the hive, it definitely got louder. Terrified the bees would try to stop her taking the spice – and even more terrified of being stung – Hattie brushed some of the fine powder into the nutshell as quickly as she could. The sweet smell of cinnamon filled Hattie's nose as much as the buzzing filled her ears.

Suddenly the buzzing was replaced by a far more threatening sound: Ivar's cackle!

Hattie glanced around in panic, but there was no sign of the Imp King.

Mith Ickle hurriedly returned to Hattie, clutching the nutshell carefully as she flew. The nutshell was just over half full. It would have to do. Though the bees were still safely inside their hives, the buzzing wasn't getting any quieter – and nor was Ivar.

Hattie carefully took the nutshell and wrapped it very tightly in a big leaf, making sure that the spice would not spill out, then she put it into her trouser pocket. Quickly Hattie stepped back from the hives. *Squelch!* Her trainers sent a splash of water flying into the air – closely followed by an alarmed dragon, as Mith Ickle dodged it.

'Where's all this water coming from?' asked a worried Mith Ickle.

'I think I can guess,' said Hattie, looking down.

The puddle under her feet was growing steadily. It seemed like it would soon join up with the other puddles that had appeared in the grass nearby.

'Ivar must have been behind us, creating springs while we were collecting the spice!

Come on – let's get out of here before we get bogged down. I hope the puddles don't trap any of the creatures around here.'

Mith Ickle stayed in the air as Hattie leapt across the soggy grass, past the entrance to

Dragon's Valley and back on to a dry path. They heard laughter as Hattie jumped in the smaller puddles and over the larger ones.

'It sounds like Ivar's getting closer, Mith,' Hattie said to her friend. 'We'd better hurry to the Enchanted Orchard. Can you lead me there?'

'Follow me!' said Mith Ickle, shooting off as fast as her dragon wings could carry her.

Friend or Foe?

They reached the Enchanted Orchard in no time. Hattie caught her breath and looked around her.

'Wow, this is beautiful!' she gasped.

Thousands of apples gave off a warm light, which made the shadows that fell on the ground a deep golden colour. The grass was as velvet soft as in Unicorn Meadows, but it too had a glow that lit up Hattie's trainers as they sank into it.

Hattie knew at once that finding the right tree wasn't going to be easy. All the trees had twisted branches and pale leaves, and there were hundreds of them!

Mith Ickle darted through the orchard, soon disappearing from view. Hattie, meanwhile, ran along a line of trees, desperately searching for one that stood out from the rest. She kept seeing the little dragon flitting about above her.

The apples all looked the same too. They were the shiniest and rosiest Hattie had ever seen, tempting her to pick one and take a bite.

They looked like they'd be the sweetest apples she'd ever taste!

When she reached the far corner of the orchard, Hattie heard a soft giggling and realized that they weren't alone. Mith Ickle flew up behind her and Hattie brought her finger to her lips, signalling to her friend to keep quiet.

Creeping forward, Hattie peered round a tree trunk.

She couldn't believe her eyes! There under an apple tree was a boy, happily juggling several shiny red balls.

But I'm supposed to be the only human in Bellua! thought Hattie, a little confused.

She slowly crept closer. She was just a few steps away when she realized he wasn't human after all. Although he had a boy's head, arms and body, below his waist he had the legs of a goat. On closer inspection she could see horns protruding from his head. And they weren't balls he was juggling but shiny red apples.

'Hey!' said Hattie. 'What are you doing?'

The goat-boy stopped juggling at once and gave her a friendly wave.

'Hi, you must be Hattie,' he said. 'I've heard all about you. I'm Billy. I'm a faun, in case you were wondering. Half-boy, half-goat. I should be called a "boat" really!'

Billy giggled at his own joke and Hattie couldn't help smiling too. Mith Ickle, however, gave an unimpressed *'Humph!'* and blew out a puff of hot smoke.

'Did you pick those apples?' Hattie asked.

Billy shook his head. 'I found them on the grass. Look – they even have bruises from where they fell.'

He held one up to demonstrate before starting to juggle again. He threw the apples higher and then lower, over and under each other, and even behind his own back. Hattie watched with delight until she heard the flap of Mith Ickle's wings behind her.

'Come on, Hattie. We can't waste time watching him show off. There are loads of trees we haven't checked.'

'Which tree are you looking for?' asked Billy, ignoring Mith Ickle.

Hattie wasn't sure how much to tell this seemingly friendly but unfamiliar creature. Revealing only as much information as necessary, she described the tree she was looking for.

'I think I know which one you mean,' said Billy confidently. 'Follow me!'

Hattie felt like she had followed Billy around the orchard at least twice before he stopped at a tree that was standing a little apart from the others. At first Hattie didn't think it was much different from the other trees in the orchard. Its wide, pale leaves hung from branches that were as thin as spaghetti – and almost as twisted as a bowlful of it! The branches must have been stronger than they looked because heavy red apples hung from them.

When Hattie looked back at the other trees, she realized that *this* tree really was twistier than all the others. And its leaves were the palest green she'd ever seen.

'The Great Twister Tree! It has to be!' cried Hattie. 'Thank you, Billy! You've saved Mith and me so much time. That's just what I need!'

Billy grinned. 'At your service, Guardian.'

Hattie stood on her tiptoes to get a better view. At the top of the tree, one apple stood out from all the others. It was bigger and it sparkled as if it was made of gold glitter.

'There it is at the top! That's the twistabout apple!' Hattie cried. 'I'm going up. Wish me luck!'

She jumped up and wrapped her hands round the lowest branch of the tree. Then she pulled herself up and reached for the next branch. She was getting closer and closer to the twistabout apple . . .

Then something caught her eye among the dense leaves above her – a flash of blue hair. That could only mean one thing: Immie, King Ivar's helper!

'Don't bother climbing up. You'll never get to that apple before me!' called the blue-haired imp.

'Oh, yes I will!' replied Hattie, wrapping both her legs tighter round the tree's trunk and preparing to move again.

Hattie quickly clambered up through the branches, determined not to lose the precious apple. It was the only thing that would cure Archie's hoof! However, as she climbed higher, her clothes kept getting caught on the twisty branches, slowing her down. Immie, being smaller, was moving much faster. Hattie struggled to keep up, despite Mith Ickle and Billy shouting out helpful directions from below.

She kept her eye firmly on the golden apple at the top, but with all the movement in the tree it was rocking dangerously to and fro.

'The apple!' she cried. 'It's going to fall and get bruised!'

Seconds later, Hattie was startled to see an apple sail past her shoulder. Then she saw another bounce down . . . It landed on Immie's head, knocking her right out of the tree!

Horrified, Hattie looked up. Thank goodness! The special twistabout apple was still there.

'Ouch!' Immie howled, picking herself up off the ground and rubbing her head. 'Keep your stupid apple, Hattie B! You still won't stop King Ivar. Nobody can!'

Then she stomped off, still muttering angrily, while Hattie and her friends laughed loudly.

Their delight didn't last long. Hattie had just begun to climb again when the leaves of a neighbouring tree began to rustle.

'Watch out, Hattie!' cried Mith Ickle.

Shedding his leafy camouflage, King Ivar's pointed ears and sharp features appeared before the shocked Guardian and her friends.

'Useless servant!' bellowed Ivar in the direction of the still-snivelling Immie. 'If *you* can't stop that meddling Guardian, I can!'

Hattie froze. She had to beat Ivar to that apple!

In a Whirl

The song that started to come from Ivar's thin lips was hardly tuneful, but Hattie knew exactly what he was doing. He was trying to send her to sleep with the song of the dragon. Hattie found herself yawning and her eyes began to droop almost immediately. She couldn't even try sticking a finger in each ear to drown out the sound because she had to hold on to the tree.

Hattie looked towards Mith Ickle in desperation. Her friend's face was fixed in an angry scowl. She knew it really upset the dragon to see Ivar using her power in this way.

Then Mith Ickle began to sing a tune that was far more melodic than Ivar's, and twice as loud. Billy joined in enthusiastically too, so that soon Hattie could barely hear Ivar's song at all. Instantly feeling more energetic, she climbed several branches higher, her eye still fixed on the golden twistabout apple at the top of the tree.

Snorting angrily, Ivar stopped singing.

Hattie braced herself for whatever he would try next.

Lifting both arms, he pointed his long bony fingers in her direction and cackled menacingly.

Hattie grabbed on to the tree tighter than ever and waited nervously.

The flash of light that Ivar sent towards her was so bright it lit up the entire Great Twister Tree. The leaves glowed fluorescent green and the apples shone like precious stones.

For a moment, Hattie could see only spots of light dancing in front of her watering eyes. Scrunching them tightly closed, she managed to avoid the next flash, and several more after that, but she didn't dare move a muscle until she felt Mith Ickle's warm breath on her neck.

'It's OK, you can open your eyes again,' whispered the dragon. 'I think Ivar's used up all his light power for now. That last flash hardly lit up the end of his horrible skinny fingers!'

Hattie saw that Mith Ickle was right. Ivar had tucked his arms inside his oversized cloak and seemed to be planning his next move. She hoped he was tired out from all the magic he'd used. She began to quickly climb through the tree branches again, hoping to reach the golden apple before he recovered.

Just one branch more and she'd be there – but not if Ivar had his way. Hattie watched with dread as the evil imp rose into the air, his tiny wings flapping frantically. He was going to get the twistabout apple!

'What can I do?' Hattie called down to her friends.

She was about to lose all hope when she heard Billy yelling below her.

'Here, Hattie – catch this!' he shouted, and he threw an apple up to her. Hattie caught it firmly in one hand. 'It's a wishing apple. Take a bite and make your wish!'

There was no time to lose. Hattie bit down and wished hard. *Don't let Ivar reach the twistabout apple. Don't let Ivar reach the twistabout apple!*

As she swallowed the crisp flesh of the apple,
Hattie nervously watched Ivar fly nearer and
nearer to the glittering fruit.

'It's no use! I'm too late!' cried Hattie.

Ivar cackled as he stretched his bony fingers out for the twistabout apple, his hungry eyes flashing with glee. But then something strange happened. The branch holding the apple swerved out of his way.

Hattie couldn't feel any wind, and the other branches stayed completely still. Her wish must have worked!

Every time Ivar swooped to take the apple, the branch dodged him. The Imp King got more and more angry as the branch led him into a hopeless game of cat-and-mouse.

Billy whooped and shouted, 'You did it!' Even Mith Ickle looked impressed.

Hattie sat in the tree, grinning from ear to ear. However, they hadn't seen the last of Ivar's attempts.

When Hattie felt a light breeze catching around her, she knew he had one more trick up his sleeve.

Out of Reach

From her branch, Hattie watched as Ivar began to circle the Great Twister Tree. The leaves rustled as his long cloak trailed behind him. He went round the tree twice more and the branches began to sway. Hattie had to grip on more tightly. He was using the power of the unicorn's horn to whip up a storm, just as he had when he had hurt the young pegasus!

The breeze gradually grew stronger. As Ivar continued to circle the tree, faster and faster, the branches rose and fell, and Hattie was stuck holding on to the trunk. The wind whipped her hair round her face, and Hattie's fingers began to lose their grip. The tree started swaying dangerously from side to side, and Hattie slipped, only just managing not to fall.

'Hold on tight, Hattie!' called Billy from below.

The faun's face was fixed in a worried frown as he darted around, ready to catch Hattie if she fell. Beside him, Mith Ickle hovered nervously, shooting out puffs of smoke and flame whenever Ivar passed her, to try to send him off course.

However, the wind showed no signs of stopping. Just when Hattie was feeling at her most desperate, she was dismayed to see Billy suddenly leave. He galloped through the orchard until he was out of sight completely.

'Where's Billy gone?' Hattie called to Mith Ickle, as Ivar whipped up an extra-strong gust of wind.

Mith Ickle smiled reassuringly up at her. 'Don't worry – he'll be back. Keep holding on, Hattie!'

The little dragon was right. After less than a minute Billy reappeared, dashing through the trees and holding a long horn.

What's that? wondered Hattie.

She watched as Billy put the horn to his lips and blew as hard as he could. His cheeks turned bright pink as a shrill trumpet sound echoed through the orchard. It was so loud that even Ivar covered his ears with his hands. Hattie, though, didn't dare let go of the tree trunk.

It took three blasts on the horn before Hattie saw the effect. A dull thud of hooves galloping on the soft orchard grass was followed by the appearance of two creatures: Themis and Arlon, who arrived as if by magic.

Even Ivar seemed stunned by their arrival. For a moment, he flew erratically round the tree, and Hattie thought the wind had begun to die down. Then suddenly there was a huge gust and she had to use all her strength to hold on.

Arlon reacted immediately. He unfolded his huge wings and, within seconds, was gliding through the air in hot pursuit of Ivar.

Hattie felt a lot safer now, knowing that Themis and Arlon were here to help, and she relaxed her grip on the tree. She watched in awe as Arlon chased the Imp King. The wind Ivar had created was feeble against the power of Arlon's wings, and the pegasus soon caught

up with the nasty imp, whose tiny wings were no match for Arlon's wide wingspan. As Arlon pushed Ivar further and further away from the Great Twister Tree, Hattie heard Billy calling from below.

'Go for it, Hattie!' he shouted.

'Yes – grab the apple while you can!' added Mith Ickle, fluttering towards Hattie.

Glancing up, Hattie could still see the twistabout apple glinting above her.

Meanwhile, Ivar was struggling to control his flight as he faced Arlon a few metres away.

Without hesitating, Hattie turned and scrambled up the Great Twister Tree as quickly as she could until the apple was within reach.

The apple shimmered brightly when she
finally wrapped her fingers round it and gently
tugged it loose. With a beaming smile, Hattie
pushed the apple into her pocket, where it
glowed through the material. Then she began
climbing gently down through the branches.

Hattie was halfway down the tree when she realized that Arlon had landed on the ground below her, and Ivar was nowhere to be seen — but her relief didn't last long.

A tell-tale cackle echoing through the orchard told her he hadn't gone far. Hattie froze as the cackle turned into a roar so loud it made Hattie and all the gathered creatures jump. Then Ivar's voice rang out through the trees, more threatening than ever.

'*That twistabout apple will not leave this orchard! Oh, you foolish Guardian, beware the mighty Ivar! Beware! Beware!*'

Apple Attack!

'Hattie! Watch out!'

Billy's cry made Hattie spin round. She was just in time to see Ivar hurtling towards her, his face twisted in rage.

'Give me that apple!' he spat, lunging forward and extending a spindly arm in her direction.

Hattie ducked, and Mith Ickle curled herself protectively round her shoulders. With a loud snort, Themis reared up on his hind legs. Then the majestic unicorn charged towards Ivar, causing the squealing imp to spring back in terror.

Within seconds, though, the Imp King was back. This time Ivar swooped towards Hattie from above. He flapped his wings as fast as he could and zoomed all around her, stretching out his bony arms as he tried to grab the apple. Hattie batted him away, but she could see he wasn't going to give up easily.

As soon as Ivar came dangerously close to her, Themis sprang into action again. The unicorn galloped round the Great Twister Tree so that the determined imp had no hope of getting close enough to take the precious apple from Hattie's pocket.

Snarling with frustration, Ivar retreated behind the trunk of a nearby tree.

Hattie knew she needed to find a way to get rid of the wicked imp once and for all. Glancing around, she had an idea. She grabbed a large apple from the branch next to her. Then, using all her might, she threw it right at Ivar – and was delighted to hit her target on the shoulder!

Encouraged by her success, and Themis's and Arlon's shouts of congratulation, Hattie grabbed apples from every branch she could reach and threw them at Ivar as hard as she could. When she ran out of apples, Mith Ickle came to the rescue, flying to the higher branches and delivering more apples into Hattie's hands.

'Try these, Hattie,' called Billy, throwing some yellowy-orange apples to her from a short, squat tree that was heavily laden with fruit. 'They're bouncer apples. Watch!'

Billy threw an apple at the ground, and Hattie watched it spring towards Ivar, who only just managed to jump out of the way in time.

'Brilliant!' cried Hattie, taking the first of the bouncer apples in her hand and hurling it at Ivar. 'Mith, Billy – join in!'

As more and more apples hit him, the Imp King's roars of fury were soon replaced by yelps of pain. Then, as though someone had given them a silent signal, all three friends threw an apple at the same time. One hit Ivar's leg, another smacked into his chest and the third bounced off his bottom.

'Yow, ow, ouch!' cried Ivar, hopping on his injured leg and rubbing his sore body. 'Immie! Immie! Where are you, you useless servant? Help me, worthless imp! NOW!'

At this, Hattie saw the blue-haired imp emerge from behind a clump of grass, her eyes full of fear.

'What shall I do, Your Majesty?' she said in a tiny, shaky voice.

'Just – just – oh, just come with me, you pathetic imp!' huffed Ivar, before turning back towards Hattie. 'You won't get away from me again, Guardian!' he spat, wagging a long thin finger at her. 'You or your pathetic friends. Soon you won't have any friends anyway. When *I* am the supreme leader of Bellua, no creature will listen to you. They will all be under MY command. There will be no place for you in Bellua – EVER AGAIN!'

Hattie felt Mith Ickle settle round her shoulders, the dragon's warm little body trembling as Ivar blustered on.

'I know which creature will give me the ultimate power,' he continued, narrowing his mean eyes, 'and I know where to find her. Nothing will stop me in my quest. NOTHING! So beware, meddling Guardian. This is not the last you'll see of me, be certain of that!'

As Ivar limped away, his cloak swishing behind him, Hattie didn't doubt his threat for a moment. Feeling suddenly exhausted from climbing trees and throwing apples, she sank to the ground.

When she looked up, she saw Mith Ickle, Billy, Themis and Arlon gazing at her sympathetically.

'Thanks so much for helping me out,' she said. 'Ivar's getting more and more determined. I wish I knew which creature he's after next. Maybe we could try to stop him now, before he even . . .' Hattie's voice trailed off as she remembered Archie waiting for her to return and cure his twisted hoof. 'We need to get back to Unicorn Meadows right now. Come on, everyone – we'd better hurry up. Ivar will have to wait!'

Then, though her legs were quite wobbly, Hattie jumped up. Billy put out one arm to steady her.

'You are in no state to hurry anywhere, young Guardian,' said Themis in a kindly voice.

'I . . . I'm fine,' replied Hattie. 'I have to get back to Archie. He needs me!'

'Then let me take you,' said Arlon, bowing his long neck towards her. 'Climb on!'

Encouraged by Mith Ickle and Billy, Hattie gratefully swung her leg over Arlon's back. Themis gently nudged her with his nose until she had shuffled right up on to the pegasus.

'Hold on tight, Hattie!' said Arlon, as Hattie threw her arms round his strong neck.

'We'll see you in Unicorn Meadows!' called Mith Ickle, who was already in the air and flapping her wings for a head start. Billy looked ready to set off too.

'Gather your strength during the ride, Hattie,' said Themis. 'Arlon will take great care of you.'

Hattie felt a cool breeze as the pegasus spread his wide wings and leapt gracefully from the ground. They soon left Themis behind them, and the trees of the Enchanted Orchard were just a blur of green below. All around her, the Belluan sky glimmered and glittered.

No fairground ride could ever be this magical, thought Hattie.

As Arlon soared towards Unicorn Meadows, his passenger looked upon the magical Kingdom of Bellua, her eyes wide with wonder.

Stepping Out

It didn't take long to reach Archie. He was resting on a clump of emerald-green grass by the arch to the Valley of the Guardians. Beside him, his mother softly nuzzled her young son.

Arlon landed gently beside them and lowered his neck so that Hattie could easily slide off. He greeted his family warmly, but looked concerned about Archie.

'Mum said you would be back soon,' whispered Archie, smiling weakly.

'I came as quickly as I could,' said Hattie, putting her hand on Archie's fuchsia mane. 'Now come with me. I promise I'll look after

you and bring you back to your family as soon
as I can.'

The little limping pegasus said goodbye to
his parents, and Hattie led him back to the cave,
with Mith Ickle and Billy hurrying behind.

Inside the cave, Hattie found a red-and-blue-
checked blanket hanging on an old wooden
hook and spread it on the hard stone floor.
She settled Archie on it, where he curled
up gratefully, with Billy and Mith Ickle
watching over him. Hattie quickly looked at
the red book again, then began carrying out
the instructions.

She found a sharp knife in the bowl of instruments on the stone table and a small wooden board propped up on one of the cave shelves. She halved the apple then sat down next to Archie. As she carefully cut the first thin slice,

her eyes widened in wonder. The flesh of the apple had a golden glow, which was bright enough to be reflected in Archie's apricot coat.

When she sprinkled the cinnamon spice on to the twistabout apple, the glow became even brighter, so that the crystal-encrusted walls of the cave twinkled. It looked even more magical than usual! Hattie hoped the apple's healing effect would be just as powerful.

'Here, take a bite,' Hattie urged Archie, holding out the slice.

As Archie began to nibble, Hattie saw his twisted hoof make the smallest of movements. She held out the slice again. 'Can you eat the whole piece? I think it's going to work!'

The young pegasus didn't need much encouragement. With each bite he took, Hattie could see his injured hoof recovering. After several slices, Archie was almost completely better. Hattie sprinkled a little extra cinnamon spice on the final piece for luck. Then she put the leftover spice in a small jar and added it to the collection of potion bottles on the cave shelves.

Hattie breathed a sigh of relief as she watched a broad smile spread across her young patient's face.

'You've fixed it, Hattie! You've fixed it!' Archie cried, jumping up and testing out his healed foot.

'Slowly, slowly!' laughed Hattie. 'Take a couple of steps with me first.'

Together they circled the stone table twice before Hattie felt Archie was ready to attempt walking on his own. Although his first solo steps were a bit wobbly, Archie was soon walking steadily. He got faster and faster, until he looked like he might break into a gentle trot!

'Whoa, steady!' said Billy, as he jumped out of Archie's way. 'Do you think you've got all your powers back in your hoof now?'

Archie stamped his foot on to the cave floor with a loud *CLOP*. A spring of water shot up and sent Mith Ickle flapping into the air with

an annoyed screech. Though Billy managed to leap out of the way in time, Hattie was too slow to avoid taking an unexpected shower – much to the amusement of her friends!

'Sorry, Hattie,' said Archie, looking sheepish as water dripped from Hattie's nose. 'Guess I still need to practise that a bit.'

Then he tapped his hoof more gently and a much smaller spring appeared. Every drop of water in it shimmered like a beautiful diamond, which vanished with a tiny spark as it hit the cave floor. When the spring had disappeared, instead of a puddle Hattie saw a glinting pegasus charm.

Hattie picked up the charm and attached it to her bracelet straight away.

'Thanks, Archie,' she said with a smile. 'I'd better get you back to your family now. Let me just put my special red book away and we'll head back outside.'

'OK, Hattie,' said Archie. Then, as Hattie was closing the book, he flapped his tiny wings and managed to lift himself into the air.

'Hey, I thought you weren't supposed to try flying until you're older!' laughed Hattie, as Archie smiled sheepishly. She returned the

book to its place on the shelf and then said to her friends, 'Come on – let's get going.'

'I can take Archie for you,' offered Billy, as Hattie made her way towards the cave door. 'You should get out of Bellua in case Ivar decides to visit again.'

'Hmm, I think you might be right,' said Hattie, looking out of the window nervously. 'Thank you for all your help today, Billy. I'm sure I'll see you again soon. Ivar meant it when he made that threat about getting the ultimate power.'

'Anytime,' replied Billy, as he guided Archie towards the cave door. 'I'm always happy to help – you only have to ask.'

'Me too,' added Mith Ickle, swooping down on to Hattie's shoulder and nuzzling her neck. 'Just as I've always been.'

'Yes, I couldn't have got this far without you,' agreed Hattie fondly. Then she and Mith Ickle called a friendly goodbye to Billy and Archie, and watched them head back to Unicorn Meadows.

'Time for me to go too,' said Hattie, reaching for the vet's bag that would take her back to the real world. 'Bye, Mith – and take care. I'll need my friends on my next visit. It doesn't look like Ivar's going to give up without a fight!'

Just mentioning the nasty imp made his parting words ring in Hattie's ears: *Nothing will stop me in my quest. NOTHING!*

However, knowing that all her friends would be there to help her, Hattie put Ivar out of her mind. Then she peered into the bag and began her familiar tumble back home.

A Sporting Chance

Once back in her room, Hattie quickly shoved the vet's bag under her bed and reached for a hairband on her bedside table. Since she'd told Chloe she was going to get one, she thought she should at least come back with her hair tied back! Then she hurried downstairs, out of the front door and back to school.

No time had passed in the real world while she had been in Bellua. So back on the sports field everyone was just starting to form into groups, depending on what they wanted to practise.

'Ah, there you are!' said Chloe, who was about to pick a small red ball from a net bag. 'I'm going to do some throwing practice, like I said. How about you?'

'I might try that too,' said Hattie, reaching for a ball herself.

'But I thought you hated throwing?' Chloe's eyebrows were raised in surprise.

'Well, maybe I'm not as bad at it as I thought,' replied Hattie. Then she added a little mysteriously as she stretched her throwing arm: 'I've had a bit of practice lately.' She would never forget the Guardian's secret oath, even though she was itching to tell Chloe all about what had happened in the Enchanted Orchard.

Just then, Mr Kennedy blew his whistle. Hattie followed her group and lined up to take her turn. When it came, she grasped the ball firmly, raised her arm and threw as hard as she could.

'Oh, Hattie!' laughed Chloe, as the ball curved so far to the left that another group of children had to duck to avoid it.

With a laugh, Hattie decided she must be more suited to throwing apples!

When Hattie and Chloe emerged from the girls' changing room after Sports Club, they discovered a huddle of children in the playground all talking excitedly.

'I wonder what's going on there?' asked Hattie, as she and Chloe wandered over.

In the middle of the crowd, Rishi was smiling happily, while several of their classmates gave him friendly pats on the back.

'You're in our team for football tomorrow then?' a boy called Leo was saying.

'And you'll come to the hockey trials next week?' asked a blonde girl called Josie.

'Your running's awesome! We should have a race sometime,' said a boy who Hattie knew was one of the fastest runners in the school.

'Looks like Rishi's settling in pretty well,' said Chloe. 'It's just as well he made it to Sports Club. No thanks to Victoria.'

Hattie and Chloe had reached the school gate when they heard footsteps behind them. Rishi appeared at their side.

'Thanks for helping me out before,' he said with a smile. 'It's nice to know that most of the kids are friendly here.' Then he called goodbye as he jogged away.

At the crossroads near the school, Hattie and Chloe said goodbye as they set off for home. Hattie was taking her usual route down the village high street when a cheery 'hello' caught her attention.

Looking up, she spotted Uncle B coming out of the greengrocer's. In his hand he was clutching a brown paper bag.

'Ah, Hattie, would you like an apple? I've heard you like them, and these are lovely and sweet.'

Then, without waiting for his niece to reply, Uncle B tossed a shiny red apple towards her – and, to her surprise, Hattie caught it perfectly!

'Got to dash,' said Uncle B. Then he added with a wink, 'Enjoy your apple, won't you? Cheerio!'

Hattie bit into the crisp fruit. Uncle B was right – it was the sweetest apple she'd ever tasted.

By the time Hattie got home, all that was left of the apple was the core. As she tossed it expertly into the bin, the charms swinging side by side on her bracelet caught her attention.

There were six of them, now that she'd added Archie's pegasus charm.

Hattie knew she had to keep a close eye on them. At the first sign of a glow, she would have to hurry back to Bellua. She was more ready than ever to face King Ivar. She had to save the magical kingdom for the sake of all the creatures who lived there. Old friends, new friends and those she had yet to meet – Hattie knew she could rely on them all when the call came again.

Hattie's going to need help from all her friends in her next adventure. Turn the page for a sneak peek . . .

Hanging Out

It was a sunny Friday afternoon, and Hattie Bright and her best friend, Chloe, were sprawled on Hattie's bed, surrounded by a pile of magazines.

'Another week of school over,' sighed Hattie happily. 'I can't wait for two whole days of chilling out!'

'Me neither,' agreed Chloe. 'It was really nice of your mum to invite me for tea today too.'

'Perfect end to the week!' said Hattie.

She turned on the stereo on her bedside table and selected her favourite song. A happy beat filled the room. The two girls jumped off the bed and began dancing around, as if they were shaking off a whole week's worth of schoolwork.

As the song finished, Chloe did a crazy spin, and both girls ended up in a giggling heap on the floor.

'Ouch, you're on my wrist!' laughed Hattie, whose right arm was pinned beneath her friend's leg.

'Is that what it is? Sorry!' said Chloe, giggling and rolling to one side.

'Too much dancing,' replied Hattie, As she said that, she could feel a funny warm tingling feeling creeping up her other arm.

Chloe got up and slotted Hattie's MP3 player into the stereo, choosing another song, and Hattie glanced at her left wrist, where she always wore her favourite charm bracelet. All six charms were swinging gently. And, just as Hattie suspected, they had started to glow a warm yellowy-orange. Hattie's stomach lurched. She wasn't sure if it was nerves or excitement, but she was certain of one thing: the evil Imp King Ivar had stolen another power from one of the animals in the magical Kingdom of Bellua. That meant they needed her there . . . now!

As Guardian of Bellua's magical creatures, only Hattie could cure Ivar's latest victim. Not only that but when she last left Bellua the Imp King had threatened the next power he would steal was going to be 'the ultimate one', stronger than any of the five he'd taken already!

Hattie shivered. Had Ivar succeeded in his quest? Would it finally be impossible to defeat him? There was only one way to find out. She had to go to Bellua right away! But how could she grab the old vet's bag hidden under her bed *and* let it secretly transport her to Bellua when Chloe was right there in the room?

Hattie knew she couldn't wait until Chloe went home after tea – that would be leaving it dangerously late. She squeezed her eyes tightly shut.

Think, think! she said to herself.

There had to be a way to get to Bellua and still keep the secret oath. Hattie only needed Chloe to leave the room for a few minutes – long enough to go to Bellua and return as if nothing had happened.

'I love this one, don't you?' said Chloe, as a new song burst from the stereo. She began dancing around the bedroom again. 'Come on, Hattie. On your feet, lazybones!'

But Hattie stayed right where she was on the bedroom floor.

'Er, actually I don't know if I do like this one that much – and anyway it's probably

nearly time for tea. Can you go down and ask my mum when it'll be ready while I choose another song?'

'OK then,' agreed Chloe, smiling at Hattie. 'But I'm trusting you to make a good choice!'

Hattie quickly jumped up and busied herself with the stereo, while Chloe slipped out of the room and headed downstairs.

With her heart pounding, Hattie hurried to her bed and reached under it. She pulled the bag out of its hiding place, dropped it on to the bed and sat down next to it. From downstairs she could hear the muffled voices of Chloe and her mum.

As fast as she could, she pressed the glowing star charm on her bracelet against the bag's star-shaped lock. It clicked open immediately and, as the bag began to sparkle and shimmer, Hattie strained her ears for any sound of Chloe making her way back up the stairs. Was that a creak?

Hattie didn't have time to check. She grasped the bag firmly and pulled it wide open. Then she peered inside and found herself tumbling down, down and down . . .

'Your mum says tea's in ten minutes, Hattie!' called Chloe as she pushed the bedroom door open. 'Hattie? Hattie, where are you?'

Chloe glanced towards the silent stereo, then at Hattie's empty bed. What was that sparkly silver bag lying on it? Chloe couldn't remember seeing Hattie with it before. Moving nearer, she looked at the bag more closely, then gasped as she took in the strangest sight she'd ever seen – Hattie's blue trainers disappearing inside!

'H-Hattie?' whispered Chloe, her voice trembling. 'A-are you i-in there?'

Chloe knew the question was ridiculous and wasn't surprised when there was no answer. With shaking hands, she picked up the bag and looked inside. Suddenly she had the strangest sensation. Her whole body tingled and she felt as though she was being pulled into the bag by something invisible.

Then, all of a sudden, she too was tumbling down, down and down . . .

Hattie B
Magical Vet

Find out more about

Hattie B

and the creatures

from the

Kingdom of

Bellua

by visiting

www.worldofhattieb.com

Your story starts here . . .

Do you **love books** and
discovering new stories?
Then **www.puffinbooks.com**
is the place for you . . .

- Thrilling adventures, fantastic fiction
and laugh-out-loud fun

- Brilliant videos featuring your favourite authors
and characters

- Exciting competitions, news, activities,
the Puffin blog and SO MUCH more . . .

www.puffinbooks.com